Mama's Work Shoes

words by
Caron Levis

pictures by
Vanessa Brantley-Newton

Abrams Books for Young Readers
New York

Perry knew all of Mama's shoes.

The *swish-swush* shoes were for yawning, stretching, reading, drawing, and cooking.

The *zip-zup* shoes were for running, jumping, skipping, swinging, and fixing.

Flap-flip shoes were for
sunny times,

stomp-stamp shoes were
for snowflake times,

and *pat-put* shoes were
for puddle times.

No shoes were for bath time, bedtime, and tickle time.

But one morning, Mama put on a pair of shoes Perry had never heard before.
Click-clack, click-clack, click-clack.

Perry liked the sound of Mama's new shoes.
She wondered what they were for.

Click-clack, Mama made lunch right after breakfast!

Click-clack, Mama packed one lunch into a big, floppy brown bag.

She packed the other lunch into a little polka-dot bag.

Click-clack, Mama put on her jacket.

She helped Perry put on her jacket and her *zip-zup* shoes.

"Today, we are starting the new routine," said Mama.

"New?" Perry wondered if it would be shiny-slide new or itchy-shirt new.

Mama and Perry walked down the block to Nan's house.

Click-clack, click-clack, click-clack.

Perry knew about Nan's house.

Nan's house was Perry calling "*knock-knock!*"

and Nan singing "*cuckoo clock!*"

Nan's house was the *squeak-squeak* door.

Nan's house was just socks. *Slish*, *slish*, and *slide* on the shiny floor.
But today, Mama's *click-clack* shoes stayed on.
"Today, you will get to stay and play at Nan's place, while I go to
my workplace. Then I will '*knock-knock*, cuckoo clock,' and we'll
go home together. Just like we talked about, remember?"
Perry did not remember.

Mama squeezed Perry in an extra-long hug.
She smoothed Perry's already-brushed hair and wiped her already-clean face.
Mama's smile looked wiggly.
Perry's tummy felt wiggly, too.

Then Mama gave Perry a big *smooch-smack* kiss, said
"I love you, Perry-Berry," and *click-clack, click-clack,*
click-clack, she went out the door.

Perry did not like this at all.

She stomped, she kicked, she cried, "*MAMMMMMMMMMAAAAAA!*"

Perry slumped and stared, frowned and glared at the *squeak-squeak* door.
She didn't move when Nan said, "She'll be back."
She didn't move when Nan tickled her neck.

She didn't move when Nan did the
shimmy-shugga-shake-shake dance.

Well, she smiled.
And she giggled.

Then Perry *shimmy-shugga-
shake-shaked*, too.

Perry and Nan played all day.
Then "*knock-knock*," Mama was back! Perry sang "Cuckoo clock!"
and she and Mama went home.

But the *click-clack* shoes came home with them.
They would take Mama to work again tomorrow.
At dinnertime, Perry made things go away, too. *Split-splat*.

At story time, every time Mama
got to the end of a book,
Perry said, "Again, again, again!"

And when Mama said goodnight,
Perry wouldn't let go.

The next day, Perry knew what she had to do.

She hid those *click-clack* shoes.
She hid all the shoes, just in case.

But Mama found them.

"NO!" cried Perry. "NO GO-AWAY SHOES!!!"

"Oh, Perry-Berry," said Mama. "In the morning, these are my go-to-work shoes." *Click–clack, click–clack, click–clack.*

"But in the afternoon, they turn into my hurry-home-to-you shoes. Watch."

Click–clack, click–clack, click–clack. Mama walked right back to Perry.

"Run," said Perry. "Mama, run."

So Mama showed Perry how she would run home, *click-clack* fast.

"More fast!" said Perry.

Mama ran as fast as she could. *Clickity-clackity*, *clickity-clackity*, *clickity-clackity*,

fast, fast, faster . . .

. . . until Perry laughed, Mama swooped, and they collapsed into cuddles.

"No matter what shoes are on my feet, I will always come back to my Perry-Berry.
On work days, my job is to hurry home to you, and your job is to have a
squishy-squeeze hug waiting for me, okay?"

So Perry practiced.
"More squeeze, please,"
said Mama.
"More, more, more."

Now, in the morning, Perry helps Mama put on her hurry-home-to-you shoes.
She picks out swishy dance-with-Nan socks.

They walk to Nan's house together.
Click-clack, click-clack. Zip-zup, zip-zup.

Perry's tummy still wiggles when
Mama hugs her goodbye.
Mama's smile wiggles, too.

But they both know that at the end of the day,
Perry's arms will wait wide open for Mama,
who will be running back *click-clack* fast . . .

. . . so Perry and Mama's feet can meet—

tickle–tickle—
together.

For the inspirational Perrin and
Susan Van Marvelous and every family
working and playing together
—C.L.

For the children who hear the sound of shoes going out into the world
to make it happen for you . . . wait . . . for they will return.
—V.B-N.

The art in this book was created with charcoal pencil drawings and colored in Corel
Painter 2018 and collaged with handmade, vintage, and scrapbook papers in Photoshop.

Cataloging-in-Publication Data has been applied for and may be obtained from the
Library of Congress.

ISBN 978-1-4197-2554-8

Text copyright © 2019 Caron Levis
Illustrations copyright © 2019 Vanessa Brantley-Newton
Book design by Pamela Notarantonio

Printed and bound in China
10 9 8 7 6 5 4 3 2 1

ABRAMS The Art of Books
195 Broadway, New York, NY 10007
abramsbooks.com